HOUGH

D0413344

Hide and Squeak

We need to turn the magic on,
We need to save the day, come on!

®
BANTAM
BOOKS

TREE FU TOM: HIDE & SQUEAK

A BANTAM BOOK 978 0 857 51156 0
First published in Great Britain by Bantam, an imprint of Random House Children's Publishers UK
A Random House Group Company.

This edition published 2013

1 3 5 7 9 10 8 6 4 2

Tree Fu Tom created by Daniel Bays.
Based on the episode 'Hide & Squeak', written by Allan Plenderleith and Douglas Wood.
TREE FU TOM word and device marks are trade marks of the British Broadcasting
Corporation and FremantleMedia Enterprises and are used under licence. TREE FU TOM
device marks © BBC and FremantleMedia Enterprises MMX. The "BBC" word mark and
logo are trade marks of the British Broadcasting Corporation and are used under licence.
BBC Logo © BBC 2012. Licensed by FremantleMedia Enterprises.

All rights reserved. No part of this publication may be reproduced, stored in a retrieval system,
or transmitted in any form or by any means, electronic, mechanical, photocopying,
recording or otherwise, without the prior permission of the publishers.

Set in Trebuchet MS Regular.

Bantam Books are published by Random House Children's Publishers UK,
61-63 Uxbridge Road, London W5 5SA

www.**randomhousechildrens**.co.uk

Addresses for companies within The Random House Group Limited can be found at:
www.randomhouse.co.uk/offices.htm

THE RANDOM HOUSE GROUP Limited Reg. No. 954009

A CIP catalogue record for this book is available from the British Library.

Printed and bound in China

The Random House Group Limited supports The Forest Stewardship Council®(FSC®),
the leading international forest certification organization. Our books carrying the FSC label
are printed on FSC® -certified paper. FSC is the only forest certification scheme endorsed
by the leading environmental organizations, including Greenpeace. Our paper procurement
policy can be found at www.randomhouse.co.uk/environment

MIX
Paper from
responsible sources
FSC® C104723

Hide and Squeak

Tom was playing hide-
and-seek with his friends.
"Come out, come out,
wherever you are!"
cried Ariela.

Ariela was a brilliant seeker.
"Found you!" she said, tapping Tom on the back.
"Easy as Chuckleberry pie!"
Tom shook his head. Usually he
was really good at this game!

Suddenly Twigs burst out of a barrel that he'd been hiding in.

"Ha ha!" he giggled. "She found you!"

"Now I've found you too, Twigs!" grinned Ariela.

Zigzoo and Squirmtum ran up to join the gang. Ariela had found them as well!

Twigs wanted to play again.

"Let's hide in the tunnels," he suggested. "Your turn to seek, Tom."

Tom asked Squirmtum to help him be the seeker. "I don't know my way around the tunnels," he explained.

Squirmtum agreed. He and Tom would look for Twigs, Ariela and Zigzoo.

"Good luck finding me!" cried Twigs. "They don't call me Mr Invisible for nothing."

He darted into the tunnels.

"Mr Invisible? He's not *that* good at hiding!" laughed Ariela.

Tom and Squirmtum covered their eyes and started to count.

1 2 3 4 5 6 7 8 9 10...

"Coming, ready or not!" called Tom.

Tom and Squirmtum made their way into the tunnels. It was dark and gloomy. "No need to be scared, with me as your guide," said Squirmtum.

Tom decided to turn on his Tree Fu Magic.

Slide to the side,
and jump right back!
Hold your hands up high . . .
Touch your nose.
Now make a pose!
Touch your knees,
and run with me!

"Look!" said Tom. "The sapstone in my belt
is glowing. Moving turned the magic on!"

The walls had glowing tubes running through
them, carrying magic sap.
"That's where all the magic in Treetopolis
comes from," said Squirmtum.
"Be careful," warned Tom, as Squirmtum rested
against a sap tube, nearly breaking it.
"We'd all be in a lot of trouble if one of those
tubes burst!"

Twigs' laughter echoed down the tunnels, "Hee hee hee!"

Twigs must be hiding nearby! Tom and Squirmtum decided to split up to look for him.

Tom followed some footprints he'd spotted on the floor. The footprints stopped, but Twigs was nowhere to be seen!

"Maybe he *is* Mr Invisible," Tom said to himself.

Twigs laughed again and Tom
spun round. He saw Twigs
hiding above him.
"There you are!" shouted Tom.
"Found again!" grinned Twigs.

Squirmtum's tunnel was dark.
He hadn't told his friends, but he was afraid of
the dark.
"Need to crank up the old spotlight," Squirmtum
whispered.
Inside his helmet, Flicker the firefly began to
glow brightly.

An echo made Squirmtum jump in fear.

BOP-BOP! BANG!

His helmet fell off and bounced down a dark hole, knocking a wobbly boulder off the wall. CRASH!

The boulder landed on a big sap tube, blocking the flow of sap, which made the whole tree shake.

"I can't fix it, it's too dark!" shouted Squirmtum, running away.

"Treequake!" yelled Twigs as he and Tom felt the rumble.

Squirmtum grabbed his friends, "We've got to get out of here!"

Tom heard Zigzoo and Ariela's voices – it sounded like they were back in the garden.

"They're safe," said Squirmtum. "Let's go!"

The treequake continued as Tom, Twigs and Squirmtum rushed outside.

Because the sap tube had been blocked, sap started bursting out of the ground.

Squirmtum tried to stop it but . . . SPLAT!

He was thrown into Rickety's pile of berries.

More and more sap flew out of the ground.
"Sap leak!" shouted Twigs. "If all the sap leaks
out then magic won't work."

Tom needed to use his Big World Magic to stop the sap leaking out.

"It's time to do the SUPER SQUEEZE spell," he said.

TREE FU GO!

Arms up in the air!
Spread your fingers, squeeze one
hand, squeeze your other hand and
squeeze your hands together.
Now clap and say
'Super Squeeze'!

Tom gathered the Tree Fu Magic power and blasted it at the holes in the ground.

"The cracks are squeezing shut!" shouted Tom. The magic was working!

Tom looked around the garden. Where were Ariela and Zigzoo?

"They must still be in the tunnels!" gasped Twigs.

Tom turned to Squirmtum.

"We've got to rescue them," he said. "Can you show us the way?"

Squirmtum shook his head. "I'm afraid of the dark," he said. "This is all my fault."

Squirmtum explained what had happened when he got scared earlier and lost his miner's helmet.

"It's OK, everyone's afraid of something," said Tom. "We'll get through it together."

Tom, Twigs and Squirmtum went back down into
the tunnels. The path was very dark.

"I'm getting scared!" said Squirmtum.

"Don't worry," said Tom. "What things do you like
best about the tunnels?"

Squirmtum thought of pretty sap tubes, smooth
walls and round holes.

"They're all still there," explained Tom.
"You just can't see them."

Squirmtum was still afraid, but he felt a
little bit better.
"OK," said Squirmtum. "Let's find Ariela
and Zigzoo."

Ariela and Zigzoo were lost.

"These tunnels are twistier than

tangled tree roots!" said Ariela.

"Oh!" yelled Zigzoo.

The frog began to slip

down a giant hole.

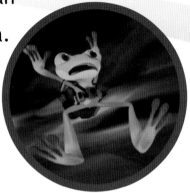

Ariela grabbed Zigzoo's arm. She tried to lasso a
root, but it was too late. The friends fell down
the hole, into a huge cavern. Zigzoo landed on
something hard.

Ariela picked it up.
"It's Squirmtum's
helmet!"
"How did it get all
the way down here?"
wondered Zigzoo.
"I guess it might have
something to do with that!" replied
Ariela, pointing to the giant blocked sap tube.
"It's getting bigger and bigger!" cried Zigzoo.
They were trapped. "Help!" they both shouted.

Squirmtum
listened hard.
"Ariela and
Zigzoo!" he
gasped. "They're
not far away."

Tom, Twigs and Squirmtum reached a ledge high
above their friends.
"Found you!" whooped Twigs.
Ariela and Zigzoo cheered - they didn't mind
losing *this* game of hide and seek.

Suddenly the tunnel began to shake. The sap tube
was going to explode!

Only Tom's Big World Magic could lift the boulder that was blocking the sap tube.

"It's time to do the SUPER LIFTO spell," he decided.

TREE FU GO!

Kneel down, hands by hips,
Crossing your body, lift one hand up,
Crossing your body,
lift the other hand up.
Now lift both hands
up together.
Super Lifto!

Tom used the magic power to lift the boulder
from the sap tube, just before it exploded.
Everyone cheered as the sap tube shrank back
to normal size.

Tom put the boulder down.

CRASH!

The bump made the ceiling of the tunnel fall
down right in front of them, blocking the way for
Tom, Twigs and Squirmtum.

How were they going to get Zigzoo and Ariela
out now?

"Any ideas, Squirmtum?" Tom asked.

Squirmtum knew another tunnel that led to the
cavern.

"It's very dark," he sighed. "Easy to get lost in."

Even though he was afraid of the dark, only
Squirmtum could rescue Ariela and Zigzoo.

Squirmtum bravely set off down the dark tunnel.

"Being in the dark is just like being in the light with your eyes closed,"

he repeated to himself over and over, just like Tom had told him to.

He slowly felt his way along.
"Everything is still the same, it's just . . . darker," he realised.
Suddenly he was in the cavern with Ariela and Zigzoo!
"Well done!" they cried.

Squirmtum had overcome his fear and
saved his friends!

Ariela had a surprise for Squirmtum.
"Here you go," she said, holding up his helmet.
"Nice to have you back, Flicker," smiled
Squirmtum.

Squirmtum led his friends back up to the garden.

"We made it!" cheered Ariela, when they reached the top.

"Thanks to you, Squirmtum," added Zigzoo.

Squirmtum felt very proud.

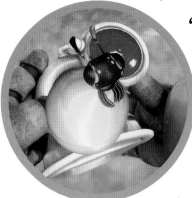

"It's all in a day's work, my friends," he boasted. He took off his helmet and lifted Flicker onto his finger.

"What a good boy you were," he cooed.

It was time for Tom to leave Treetopolis.

"Thanks for the Big World Magic," grinned Twigs.

"Thanks for a game of hide and seek that I'll
never forget!" laughed Tom.

"I've got to get back now," said Tom. "It will be dark soon."

"Dark?" joked Squirmtum. "Let me know if you need any help."

He tried his best to look big and strong, but his helmet fell off.

Tom and his friends laughed. Good old Squirmtum!